WITCH

OVER THE WATER

WITCH
OVER THE WATER

Madeline Rose
with illustrations by Trevor Weekes

ANGUS & ROBERTSON PUBLISHERS

Unit 4, Eden Park, 31 Waterloo Road,
North Ryde, NSW, Australia 2113, and
16 Golden Square, London W1R 4BN,
United Kingdom

First published in Australia
by Angus & Robertson Publishers in 1980
First published in the United Kingdom
by Angus & Robertson (UK) Ltd in 1981
This Bluegum paperback edition 1986

National Library of Australia
Cataloguing-in-publication data.

Rose, Madeline, 1932-
  Witch over the water

    ISBN 0 207 15368 X (pbk.).

    I. Title. (Series: Bluegum).

A823'.3

Printed in Australia by The Dominion Press –
Hedges & Bell

Contents

The Problem

Outside it was unfriendly and growing dark. Cold drizzling rain fell noiselessly and fog almost hid the leafless trees at the end of the long garden.

Mr Pitt came out of the rain into the warm room. He was glistening all over with raindrops.

The rim of his hat was soaked and shapeless and trickles of moisture ran down his coat and trousers and sank into the carpet. He looked so gloomy that Mrs Pitt said, "Whatever's the matter?"

The children were very busy sitting round the old-fashioned grate. The blazing coals sat in a basket of black iron bars and twelve-year-old Jean was carefully balancing chestnuts on these with a pair of long slim tongs. She pricked the nuts first with the prongs of an old broken fork, to stop them exploding, and she tried to gently turn them around when they were half done. Sometimes the chestnuts slipped off the bars and were lost in the fire. Sometimes they burned too black before she could rescue them, or she pulled them off while they still had hard waxy parts; but some of them were perfect and there

1

were lots of half successes with sweet floury centres and delicious scorched edges.

Peter, who was ten, was in charge of shelling the nuts, fumbling with a thick cloth and sometimes burning his fingers. He couldn't help making a lot of mess with the shells.

At the other side of the fire Amy was solemnly and carefully making toast with a long wire fork. It was easier than handling the chestnuts and the hot red coals toasted the slices of bread a deep golden brown.

John, Amy's twin, buttered the slices and stacked them high. He was beginning to think it was his turn to use the toasting-fork.

Mr Pitt did not answer his wife and he did not take off his dripping coat. He sat down heavily in his favourite armchair and dripped on to the cushions. So depressed was his face that Mrs Pitt was really worried.

"Why haven't you changed your school uniforms?" he said. "You'll ruin them!"

"It was the last day of term today," said their mother, "and they won't be using them again. Do tell us what's the matter. You look awful."

Mr Pitt pushed between the children and picked up the poker. He banged it angrily at a big lump of coal at the back of the grate.

"Granny Enders," he said crossly. "I called in today to say goodbye and she wants to come to Australia with us!"

Everyone looked horrified.

"But she can't!" said Jean.

"She's much too old to travel so far," said Mrs Pitt. "Besides, she doesn't like us at all and she isn't even your real mother. Didn't you tell her we were only going for three years?"

"I tried to," said Mr Pitt, "but I don't think she believed me. She just snorted in that peculiar way of hers. I also told her that we couldn't afford her passage. The firm is paying for us but I can't expect them to pay for her. And even if we had the money, the ship is fully booked. The agent told me so last week."

"It's a pity you went to see her at all," said Mrs Pitt. "She always upsets you and never seems to enjoy your visits."

"She was annoyed about the twins too," Mr Pitt went on gloomily, without appearing to hear. "We didn't send them round there on their seventh birthday last week, you know."

Their mother was angry now.

"I should think we didn't! Don't you re-member how she treated Jean and Peter on their seventh birthdays? I thought she was ill when she upset Jean like that but when it happened all over again with Peter I decided I just wasn't paying any attention to her whims again."

"Whatever are you talking about?" said Amy, wide-eyed. "What happened?"

"When I married your mother," said Mr Pitt, "Granny Enders was very much annoyed. She looked after me when I was a little boy, after my parents died in a car accident, and she thinks it gives her the right to complain about everything I do. When she saw she couldn't stop the marriage, she told me that if I had any children I must take each of them to see her on his or her seventh birthday. She said: 'They're no use till they're seven, and they won't be any good anyway, but I might as well make sure, and it's the least you can do for me!' "

"What happened when you went, Jean?" said John anxiously.

"Well, she lives up a lot of little stairs," said Jean, "and there were shelves all over the walls with hundreds of books and little jars and bottles. There were bunches of dried plants hanging on strings and a queer spicy smell."

"Go on," said Amy, curiously.

"The room was dark, with thick curtains over the windows, and she had a big green glass lamp on in the middle of the room. She called me over and turned the light full on me, then walked all round me, staring at me very hard. She took out a shiny silver tape-measure and measured my ears and fingers, and all the time she was sighing and muttering 'very disappointing' and things like that. It was awful. Then she gave me a pile of little charts covered with numbers and tiny pictures and a box full of different shapes made of coloured glass and told me to take them to the table and play with them. I was scared stiff of her but I quite enjoyed looking at the things and arranging the glass in patterns. She

4

left me alone for half an hour then came back and peered over my shoulder. Suddenly she really shouted, 'No use! No use! Just rubbish!' and she grabbed the edge of the table and threw it on its side. It made an awful crash and all the glass broke. I couldn't help crying and I ran down the stairs and all the way home."

"And you were miserable for the rest of the day," said Mrs Pitt, "and didn't enjoy your party at all. And it was just the same with Peter. I didn't want to let him go but your father thought she wouldn't be like that again."

"She wasn't always so bad-tempered," said Mr Pitt. "When I lived with her she was very kind sometimes. I expect old age is making her difficult."

Amy was dancing from foot to foot with excitement. "Do let me go and see her. I want my turn — don't you John?"

John didn't, but he couldn't lose face by admitting it. "If she's rude to me," he said, "I shall shout, 'Leave me alone you horrible old woman!'"

"That," said Mr Pitt drily, "would be very helpful!" Then he got depressed again. "I don't know what we're to do. Do you know she said if we don't take her she is going to phone my firm and tell them a sad story about being left all alone by a heartless family? They won't know that she is perfectly all right and that she won't let me go and see her more than once in six months anyway. They might even send someone else to Australia and I'm looking forward to the trip."

Mrs Pitt stood up and picked up the plate of toast which had gone quite cold. She handed it round and everyone ate absent-mindedly.

"Don't worry," she said firmly. "We are going anyway and Mrs Enders isn't going to stop us. First, let's try to make her a little more friendly. The children can all go round together. She can see the twins and they won't be afraid if the others are there. I'll make a really superb cake, or try to, and they can take it as a present. You have a few bottles of wine left, George. Send those too. You say she likes it and we don't want to take it with us. Children — when you are round there say how glad you will be to come home in three years' time. Make her understand we're not going for good. It's no use my coming — she refused ever to meet me — so you'll have to do your best. I'll make the cake tomorrow morning and you can go round in the afternoon!"

Nobody argued. Jean slipped away to her bedroom to do her homework then remembered that there was none. It was the end of term and freedom for a few weeks. The bedroom was cold and the street lights outside shone through the windows on to the piles of trunks and suitcases packed ready for Australia. Jean switched on the light and firmly drew the curtains over the glass, trying to control the feeling in her stomach. She was really afraid of seeing Granny

6

Enders again, though it seemed ridiculous.

"I mustn't let the twins know I'm nervous," she thought.

A Strange Visit

The next morning after breakfast the children helped Mrs Pitt to clear the kitchen so that she could start making the cake. Jean washed the dishes and Peter dried them. The twins scuttled around putting everything away. Somehow no one fell over anyone else and everything was tidy in an incredibly short time.

Mr Pitt put his head anxiously round the door.

"She doesn't like chocolate," he said. "She really hates chocolate cake, or anything flavoured with banana, and she dislikes cream and jam."

"What does she like then?" asked Mrs Pitt curiously.

"Spicy things," said her husband. "She always has jars of very spicy little biscuits — and nuts, she's fond of those."

"Well," said Mrs Pitt doubtfully, "I shall have to guess."

She collected together butter and sugar, flour, nuts, eggs and spices and began to make the cake. The children hung around the table watching.

"Jean — grease this tin, will you please? John, fetch the rest of those glace fruits from the dining room. We'll use them to decorate the top."

At last the cake was in the oven and it behaved beautifully. Through the glass door John and Amy watched it rise and gently brown, and it held its shape nicely as it cooled afterwards on the wire rack.

Mr Pitt brought up the wine bottles from the cellar and packed each carefully in corrugated paper before arranging them in a basket.

"This is going to be heavy," he said. "Perhaps Peter can help Jean with it."

After lunch they set off. The weather had turned colder. There was a light sheen of frost on the pavement and the leaves in the privet hedge were crisp and icy. Jean and Peter carried the wine between them. Amy had the cake in a cardboard box.

"Let me know if you get tired and I'll have a turn carrying it," said John.

Granny Enders lived about a kilometre away in a flat over a shop in the High Street. Her blue-painted door was squeezed between two shop doors. It had an intricately-twisted brass knocker.

The door was standing ajar, almost as though she was expecting them, but the stairs behind looked very dark. The children paused for a moment or two, uncertain what to do. Peter lifted the knocker and tapped and it echoed loudly on the empty stairs. There was a short silence then a deep voice, which sounded very far away, said: "Come right up, and mind you shut the door!"

There was no light at all once the door to the street was closed, but somehow they found the stairs with their feet and climbed into the darkness. It seemed much further to the top than Jean remembered.

"This is downright dangerous," she whispered to the others. "Do be careful! We could easily fall!"

"Why isn't there a rail to hold?" asked John.

"Shhh!" said Peter, feeling uneasy as he remembered his last visit. "She might be offended."

Amy was too busy to speak. She was trying to balance without dropping the cake.

At last, when all their legs ached and John was beginning to be frightened, Jean's hand touched a door across the head of the stairs. She twisted the handle and they saw the room, lit by the green lamp, bright after the darkness of the stairs.

"Come in quickly and shut the door. I can't stand draughts," said a deep, ill-tempered voice.

Granny Enders, wrapped in a green satin dressing-gown, peered angrily at them from a couch at the side of the room. She had a thin, pinched face with very bright eyes. Her hair was

10

piled high in a mass of silver curls and her thin knobbly fingers were covered with glittering rings. One foot, propped high on a pile of cushions, was encased in a very large, white plaster cast.

"Oh!" said Peter and Jean together, putting down their basket. "You've hurt yourself!"

"This was your father's fault," hissed the old lady furiously. "When he told me he wouldn't take me to Australia with you, I decided to go out and fix things. The light out there had gone and I was annoyed and in a hurry, so I fell downstairs and banged my head. If your father had closed the street door it would have been all right, but some fool saw me and called a doctor before I woke up. The idiot insisted on taking me to the hospital for X-rays and put my leg in plaster."

"But it must have needed it," said Jean in surprise, "or he wouldn't have done it. You can't go walking around on a broken leg."

"I've fixed it perfectly well myself," snapped Granny Enders. "I've had this leg for a long time and I know all about it. That fool saw it for the first time yesterday. He's put this thing on it and I can't take if off without giving myself away. It's spoilt everything!"

Jean suddenly felt very sorry for the old lady. "She's talking nonsense," she thought. "The bump on the head must have made her mind wander."

"You must rest very quietly," she said, "and try to get better. You don't realise what a shock you've had. I'm surprised they let you come home from the hospital. Who is going to look after you? Did the doctor leave you any tablets?"

"Do I look ill?" said Granny in a fury, sitting up and waving her arms around wildly. "Don't try to teach your elders and betters!"

Suddenly she seemed to notice the twins for the first time. They were trying to keep behind Peter in the shadows. "Ah! You've brought John and Amy," she said. "And about time too! Come over here you two and let me get a good look at you." She reached out her hand to the green lamp and the room grew brighter.

12

The twins came forward and looked at Mrs Enders rather nervously. The plaster-covered leg seemed to make her harmless but they were still worried about what she might say.

"Nearer — nearer — here!" she said and grabbed John by the chin. She twisted his face this way and that, peering closely at him, then she fell back against the pillows in disgust.

"No good again!" she spat. "I can tell from the start with that one! No use wasting my time."

John wasn't frightened now — he was annoyed. He meant to be polite but found himself saying, "I should think anyone you would like would be most peculiar!"

The others held their breath and waited but Granny Enders just looked hard at him then roared with harsh laughter. "Very true," she said, "very, very true. Let's have a look at your sister!"

"I'm just like John and the others," said Amy, hurriedly starting to back away. "It's really no use bothering with me."

But an arm snaked out and bony fingers grasped her wrist and pulled her to the couch. There was a long silence then the old woman actually smiled.

"Splendid!" she said in a deep, pleasant voice. "You are the very image of your father's great grandmother. I took in George thinking he had traces of her but he was a great disappointment. This is most exciting!" She waved a glittering hand at the table. "Bring me that box, Jean."

It was a small wooden box, carved all over and studded with shells. Jean picked it up and found it tremendously heavy. She carried it over to the couch and it was snatched from her.

Gently Granny Enders lifted the lid and took out a silver tape-measure, shining like a streak of light. The children craned their necks but could not see what else was in the box. Silently the old woman measured Amy's fingers and ears. "So far . . . so good!" she muttered.

"There are some things on a tray on the table over there, child," she said, almost gently. "See what you can do with them while I rest for a few minutes."

She lay back and closed her eyes, looking tired and white, and seemed to shrink against the couch. She appeared to instantly fall asleep. The children shifted uneasily from foot to foot.

"Perhaps we could sit down," whispered Jean. They tiptoed to various uncomfortable chairs around the room and perched uneasily on their edges. Only Amy remained standing by the far table and the others heard an occasional click from the little glass shapes on the tray.

"I wonder what I'm supposed to do," thought Amy, shifting the shapes and arranging the colours. "I'll probably annoy her like the others did. I wonder what she wants!"

Time passed very slowly, but just as Jean

was beginning to wonder if it would be all right if they slipped quietly away, the figure on the couch stirred and sat up again. The children watched nervously as Amy brought the tray over to show Granny Enders what she had done. The old lady bent over the shapes and patterns, for a full minute, then raised her head.

"Well!" boomed Mrs Enders, beaming at the bewildered Amy. "That's more like it! Now I shall have some help! I'd nearly given up hope." She almost chuckled in delight.

All at once the atmosphere was much friendlier. Jean was told to bring lemonade and biscuits from the carved cupboard at the end of the room, Amy suddenly remembered the cake, and in no time at all a very normal tea-party was in progress. Granny seemed relaxed and happy. She laughed and chatted and asked endless questions about their parents and the journey. She remarked rather sourly on tasting the cake that it was too sweet, but ate a large slice nevertheless.

At last she sighed and leaned back against the cushions flicking the crumbs from the rug with her beringed fingers. "And now Amy must go to the British Museum for me right away," she said.

The children looked at each other, afraid of spoiling the happy atmosphere.

"She can't, Granny Enders," said Jean, gently but firmly. "It's late and cold and foggy and the Museum is right over the other side of

London. She's too young to go by herself, anyway."

The old woman was suddenly very angry again. "She'd be quite all right," she said. "I'd see to that. What a namby-pamby set of creatures children are these days! Someone has to go there for me today or it will be too late — and it has to be Amy." She glared at them in silence for a while.

"We could go tomorrow, all together," said Peter suddenly. "Dad's taking us all over London at the weekends, saying goodbye to places we won't see again till we come back from Australia. He wouldn't mind us going to the Museum."

Mrs Enders sulked for a while then pulled a little calendar from her pocket. She stared at it with a fierce frown of concentration, then said: "Tomorrow would do — but only just. He'll still be there. Amy, I want you to go to the Egyptian Room and don't whatever you do let your father see you. Find some excuse to slip away. Look for a long frieze of men and horses with a carving of a cat at the right-hand corner. I want you to turn slowly round three times in front of that cat and say clearly, 'Mrs Enders sent me'. "

The children stared at her, astounded. "She really is mad," thought Peter. "I wonder if she's dangerous?" Then he looked at her leg and was reassured.

"The rest of you had better go with Amy," said Mrs Enders. "I'd sooner you didn't but there's nothing for it. I shall have to explain things to you sooner or later. You can keep watch and make sure no strangers come into that part of the gallery. We can't have any mistakes — there's no time."

Jean was getting more and more uneasy. She wanted to get away and talk over this nonsense with the others.

"We'll have to be going, Granny," she said hurriedly, and they all started to move towards the door.

"Don't forget now!" cried the old lady, raising herself on one elbow. "Three times! Mrs Enders sent me!"

Down the long dark stairs they fumbled and out into a cold, early twilight. They talked it over all the way home and decided that Mrs Enders must be very slightly mad.

"All the same," said John, "I think we'd better do as she says. We'll have to see her again sometime and if we have to say 'no' when she asks if we did it, she'll go into a most fearful rage."

"Yes," said Amy, who had been rather quiet. "I think we should definitely do it ... I somehow feel I have to," she finished quickly, looking a bit embarrassed. Peter looked at her curiously.

"I suppose it wouldn't do any harm," said Jean, laughing. "We'll have to see if Dad feels like the Museum."

Dad was in fact very surprised and gratified.

17

"Yes indeed," he said at the dinner table. "I like to see you taking an interest in our cultural heritage. I would very much enjoy looking at the ceramics again. It will do you a lot more good than the television and comics that seem to occupy so much of your time. We'll go tomorrow morning."

"Museums are always so interesting," murmured Jean, feeling rather guilty.

The Museum

Next morning was cold and sunny. The children laughed and talked as they walked with their parents through the grey streets and down into the Underground.

Amy loved climbing down the long flights of steps and riding on the escalators. She liked the mysterious tunnels and the rush of wind you felt as the train arrived. Today it was even better.

At last they were climbing the cold, gritty steps of the Museum.

"Where are you going?" asked Mr Pitt. "I want to look at my ceramics."

"Oh, we'll just wander around," said Jean hastily. She was afraid that her father or mother might follow them.

They set off towards the Egyptian Room. The little steel tips on John's shoes made a ringing noise on the flags. They entered the great hall and found the frieze Granny Enders had talked about without any trouble. But it was Saturday and there were lots of people in the Egyptian Room, strolling around and studying the exhibits. As the morning wore on the crowd thinned and time and again the children thought they were alone, only to be disappointed when someone else appeared. They wandered in and out, but each time they returned it was still no use.

Suddenly it was lunchtime. Their mother found them and suggested they should eat in the park as the day had become warmer. She had a basket with sandwiches, fruit, slabs of chocolate and a large bottle of fizzy orange.

It was so pleasant in the winter sunshine that they stayed there most of the afternoon. Mr Pitt dozed on a bench while Mrs Pitt read a magazine. Jean organised some games and Peter and John joined in joyfully, getting dirtier and more untidy all the time.

Everyone had a good time but Amy. She felt miserable, as though she had failed in something very important. They passed the Museum on the way home, just as it was due to close.

"Could you wait just a moment?" asked Amy breathlessly, and ran up the stone steps. After hesitating a moment the other children followed.

"Don't be long!" said a man near the door. "We close in five minutes."

They ran and ran down the corridors and paused panting before the frieze. There was no one in the room now and everything looked very still. Half the lights were out. Amy suddenly felt very foolish. She turned round three times and said in a very small voice, peering at the cat, "Mrs Enders sent me."

And then a fantastic thing happened. The cat in the frieze moved. It turned its head and looked Amy full in the eye, then it jumped down and pressed itself against her leg. It was not cold stone. It was warm and silky.

The children were so shocked they stood staring at the cat with dry mouths. The corner of the frieze was quite empty and a very real animal sat at their feet looking sharply at them.

They were not even surprised when he spoke.

"Open your basket," he said in a thin, high voice. "There's not much time!"

Jean looked down, startled, and realised she was carrying the empty lunch basket. She fumbled with the straps and the lid fell down. The cat jumped swiftly in and curled up neatly.

"Fasten the lid," he said, "and take me home with you, and don't tell anyone."

They did just that. They were so surprised

21

that they could not even talk to each other about it as they walked out of the Museum.

Amy carried the basket at first but Jean soon took it from her as it was too heavy. It was extraordinarily heavy for a cat, but then, thought Jean, in a dazed way, it was an extraordinary cat.

Their parents were walking up and down outside, stamping to keep warm.

"Why on earth did you run off like that?" asked Mrs Pitt crossly. "I'm half frozen."

All the way home in the Tube the children did not speak. They just stared at each other and wondered.

"I think you're all overtired," said their mother. "We'll have an easy day tomorrow. Shall I carry the basket, Jean?"

"No thank you," said Jean hastily. "It's quite light."

When they reached the end of their road Jean lagged slightly behind the others. Her arm ached from the weight of the basket.

Suddenly a muffled little voice spoke. "Let me out!"

She paused by a shrub where her parents could not see her and lifted the lid. A flash of fur streaked out and away into the nearest garden.

"Jean, where are you?" called her father, and she hurried on.

"It's gone!" she whispered to the other children, as they stared at her in the dusk.

They reached the house and Mr Pitt searched

his pocket and found his keys. He started to open the door, then paused, listening. Behind them there was a very faint miaow.

Everyone turned around. The cat stood there, looking pathetic, one paw dangling in front, and miaowed again.

"Goodness, it's a Siamese," cried Mrs Pitt. "I didn't know anyone had one round here ... and it's hurt! I wonder if it will come inside?"

She needn't have wondered. It came inside very readily and drank a large saucer of milk. It then curled up by the fire like any normal cat.

"What a pity we have no cat food," said Mrs Pitt. "I shall have to give it a slice off the roast."

The cat opened one eye and looked at her sarcastically.

Granny Enders Explains

After dinner Mr Pitt disappeared to his study to check details about the trip to Australia, and the currency arrangements. Mrs Pitt went to the telephone out in the hall and the children could faintly hear her talking to someone at the local police station.

The cat jumped smoothly on to the table and spoke to the children. Although it had happened before they again found themselves staring at him in stunned silence.

"You have done very well," he said calmly. "My name is Candar and we are going to get on nicely together."

He had a faintly bossy tone which worried Jean.

"Tomorrow you must take me to Mrs Enders and ... " He stopped as the door opened and as Mrs Pitt came back into the room he washed his nose with one paw, sitting silently amid the china cups.

"Well really!" she said in annoyance, scooping him up and dropping him on the rug. "I don't know what you are all thinking about, letting a cat jump on to the table like that!" The children stared at her. It had not occurred to them to treat Candar like the old ginger tom-cat from next door who sometimes wandered in and tried to steal things off the kitchen table.

The cat looked offended. He turned his back on them and stared at the fire.

"Hurry up and help me tidy the room," said Mrs Pitt. "Two people who live near here have lost Siamese cats and the police are going to contact them and give them our address."

Peter was alarmed. "How would they know if it was their cat?" he said. "There were a lot of Siamese at that cat show we went to last year, and they all looked just the same to me!"

An offended splutter came from the hearth rug.

"Of course they'd know," said Mrs Pitt. "People recognise their own pets and the cat will probably make a fuss of them too."

The first caller was a mournful little man in a grubby coat. "No that isn't mine," he said sadly as soon as he saw Candar. Amy saw him to the door feeling terribly sorry for him. "I hope you find him soon," she said.

The second cat owner arrived half an hour later. She was plump, wore a great deal of lipstick and carried a large cat basket in her hand.

"Yes, that's my animal," she said briskly, after one sharp glance at Candar. "Help me pop him in here and we won't cause you any more trouble."

The children were very worried. "Are you sure?" said Jean. "You haven't really looked at him properly yet."

"Of course!" said the woman becoming cross. She turned and glared at Jean. "I'd know those dark brown ears and tail anywhere!"

Jean flushed and was about to say that all seal-point Siamese had that colouring, when she heard the woman gasp.

Candar was sitting on the rug staring at her and his ears were snow-white . . . white to their tips.

Mrs Pitt was puzzled and uneasy. She was surprised she herself had not noticed those white ears before.

"Well, it doesn't look as if this is your cat after all," she said. "Let's see if he knows you."

Candar promptly arched his back and spat at the plump woman.

"That settles it then," said Mrs Pitt, nervously but firmly. She showed the visitor, still protesting, to the door.

"Perhaps we should have let her take him," she said afterwards. "Goodness knows what we'll do with him if we can't find him a home before we go to Australia."

John jumped up and down with excitement. "Maybe Granny Enders would like him," he said. "He'd keep her company. Can we take him round there tomorrow?"

"What ideas you have!" said Mr Pitt, coming in with a sheaf of papers. "She won't want him, I can tell you that — and how would a bed-ridden old lady look after a cat?"

But the other children were glad to see an excuse for taking the cat where he wanted to go. They argued and persuaded.

"We could buy lots of tinned cat food for him," said Jean, "and he'd be wonderful company. Perhaps she'd stop thinking about coming to Australia."

Mr Pitt didn't think that was likely but it was a straw to clutch at.

"Well ... you can take him over," he said slowly. "There's no harm in trying. Of course his owner may turn up yet. You'd better explain that to Granny. This may be a valuable cat."

For the rest of the evening the children waited anxiously for the doorbell or the telephone to ring, but everything was quiet. No one else seemed to be interested in Candar.

Next morning was cold but the sun was bright. They set off just after breakfast with the cat safely in the lunch basket.

The blue door was open again but this time the stairs behind were brightly lit. Jean opened the basket and Candar darted up the stairs. By the time they panted to the top he was sitting on the bedside table with his tail curled smoothly round his legs.

"Come in, come in children!" said Granny Enders, her voice warm with pleasure. "Sit down all of you. This is splendid!"

She ruffled Candar's fur with her bony hand

and he turned and whispered something in her ear.

"Yes, you're right," she said with a high-pitched laugh. "They're good children and they can help. Listen to me carefully, all of you! For want of a better word you can call me a witch!"

The children were not in the least surprised. After yesterday they were willing to believe anything. They were all very relieved that Mrs Enders seemed to be in a pleasant mood. Eager to hear more, they sat in a semicircle on the faded carpet, which was covered with intricate patterns of blue, red and green, and listened.

"Normally," said Mrs Enders, cracking her knuckles and rubbing her diamonds and rubies against her chin, "people like me don't grow old. But every seventy years or so we need renewing. This is done with various plants prepared in a very special way. Never before have I had any difficulty. When the time came I went into the country and found my herbs, and soon I was young and strong again. But this century . . . what do I find?"

There was a short silence.

"Has something gone wrong with the plants?" asked Amy breathlessly.

"Wrong?" screamed Granny suddenly. "I should say so! Weedkillers! Weedkillers sprayed the length and breadth of this country . . . the length and breadth of Europe! It's criminal! I left it very late this time and I've hunted for my plants for the last five years, growing weaker and weaker. That is why I must get to Australia."

"But don't they have weedkillers there?" said Jean.

"They do," said the old lady grimly, "they do! But it's a bigger place and there are fewer people. There must be parts where people haven't meddled at all yet and even if the plants are not the same there may be substitutes. I'll know them if I see them."

"If you're a witch," said John, "couldn't you just magic yourself to Australia? Couldn't you ride on a broom?"

"I'm not strong enough," said Mrs Enders pathetically. "I still have enough power to mend a broken leg but not enough to force your father to take me with you or to counterfeit the money for the fare. I can still fly — it's like riding a bicycle, you never forget it — but not for long distances. I need a base to return to. I need help and refreshment. I could fly close to the ship if Candar was on board. He has a little power of his own — just enough to boost mine. That is why you have to take him on the ship with you. Persuade your parents to take the cat and we can manage!" She rubbed her glittering hands together.

"We'll try," cried Jean excitedly. They all started talking at once. Mrs Enders pulled a paper bag from under her coverlet and handed round small, spicy biscuits.

"Oh I've just remembered!" cried Peter

suddenly. "We told Dad we were bringing Candar here to ask you if you would like to keep him."

"Well that wouldn't do at all," said Granny. "Take him home again and tell your father I can't stand animals! Get very fond of that cat. Tell your parents you'll be heartbroken if you don't take him with you."

The children looked doubtfully at Candar. He was sitting watching them with a cold, supercilious eye, but they all wanted to help.

"It might be a good idea if you made more of a fuss of Mother and Dad, Candar," said Jean cautiously. "Purr around a bit like an ordinary cat. You were a bit distant with Mother last night. You almost sneered at that milk she put down for you."

"I prefer cream," said Candar coldly. "Milk needs warming. But I'll make an effort for you, my dear!" He lightly bit the lobe of Granny Enders' ear and jumped to the floor. "Don't bother with the basket. I know the streets now and I'll make my own way back."

Candar Disappears

Both parents were out when they arrived home. The children talked it over and decided to wait a few days before asking about Candar.

"We must give them time to get fond of him," said Jean.

The cat reappeared about four o'clock, howling at a window. They rushed to let him in and he made straight for the fire and stretched out in front of it.

Mrs Pitt arrived a few minutes afterwards with cheeks pink from the cold and a basket half full of tinned cat food. She had not expected Mrs Enders to want a pet.

"There!" she said, arranging the tins in the cupboard. "That should keep him going until we find his owner. I've put an advertisement in the local paper, a notice in the pet shop window and one in the post-office."

The children, rather worried, watched Candar carefully, but he behaved perfectly. He rubbed around Mrs Pitt's legs and purred and he ate his supper, evidently grateful, except for one wry secret grimace of distaste at Peter. Afterwards he jumped lightly on to Mr Pitt's knee and settled down, purring again.

"He's making himself quite at home," said Mr Pitt, flattered. "I don't know why he isn't fretting for his real owner. Siamese generally do."

But when, several days later, the children asked if it would be possible to take Candar to Australia both parents were quite firm.

"Of course not!" said Mrs Pitt. "It would cost a great deal of money. He'd spend the trip in a little cage being thoroughly miserable, and in Australia he would have to stay in quarantine for weeks and weeks after we landed. He'd hate it! No — if his owner doesn't turn up soon we'll

advertise for a home for him. Someone is bound to want a beautiful cat like this."

Candar had been listening carefully to Mrs Pitt's description of the trip. As soon as he was alone with the children he said firmly: "That settles it! Stop trying to persuade them. I'm certainly not travelling like that."

"But what will you do?" asked Amy. "You know how important it is that you should go."

"I'll be with you," said Candar briefly. He turned his back on them, yawned and stretched out in front of the fire, seeming instantly to fall asleep. The children did not dare wake him to ask further questions.

The days went by and soon it was only a week before the sailing date. Mr Pitt came home that night looking extremely pleased. "I've solved our problem about the cat," he said joyfully, scratching Candar behind the ears. "Mrs Thorpe from the office will have him. She's a very nice person and he'll have a good home. She's coming to get him tonight."

The children looked at each other silently. They looked at Candar who seemed completely calm. All through dinner they worried and wondered. At about eight o'clock when Amy and John were bathed, dressed and ready for bed, the doorbell rang loudly.

Mrs Thorpe did look pleasant. She was a little rosy-cheeked woman and she carried a very comfortable-looking basket on one arm. "What a

33

beautiful cat," she said happily as she came into the warm sitting-room.

Quick as a flash Candar ran to the open door. He paused in the hall, glancing around, then streaked up the stairs.

"Oh dear!" cried Mrs Pitt. "Catch him, Jean!"

Jean ran up the stairs after Candar. She didn't know what she was supposed to do. He had already disappeared when she reached the landing. She went slowly from one room to the other, peering under beds and behind doors, but he was nowhere to be found.

"Hurry up Jean!" called her father from down below. "Mrs Thorpe has to catch a bus."

Jean went on to the landing and called over the bannister. "He's gone," she said. "He's just vanished."

Everyone else came upstairs and they looked in all the places Jean had already searched, but they found nothing, not a paw-print . . . not a whisker!

"What a shame!" said Mrs Pitt, crossly. "We really should have been more careful. He was nervous. He's bound to turn up soon, Mrs Thorpe, and when he does we'll bring him round to you. I'm so sorry you've had the journey for nothing."

Mrs Thorpe was not upset. She laughed and said she would look forward to meeting Candar another time. Mr Pitt put on his coat to take her to the bus-stop. The children said goodbye then ran up to Jean and Amy's room to talk things over.

"Do you suppose he's going to stow away on the boat? Where can he be now? The windows are all too high for jumping."

One wall of the bedroom was decorated with a patterned paper. It was covered with pictures of little houses with fancy iron railings. In front of each identical house was a small circular flowerbed. Small dogs, children with balloons and men on old-fashioned bicycles wandered between the houses.

Amy had always loved the paper. She lay on her back now and stared at it — then suddenly she shouted, "Look!"

On the doorstep of one of the little houses was a small Siamese cat. Hurriedly the children glanced around the wall. The other doorsteps were all empty.

"It must be him!" cried Amy, her voice squeaking with excitement.

They stared hard at the little picture. The cat was not looking at them. It was gazing calmly ahead. It was printed in just the same tones as the rest of the wallpaper and looked as though it had been there forever.

"They'll never find him there!" said Peter admiringly. "I wonder how he does it."

Many times that week they went upstairs to look at the little picture on the wallpaper.

Candar never spoke nor gave any sign. After a few days they began to wonder if they were imagining the whole thing.

Mr and Mrs Pitt were annoyed and embarrassed when they failed to find the cat. They were also upset as they had grown fond of him and were afraid he might have had an accident.

Two Different Ways to Travel

The day before they were due to sail the phone rang and Mrs Pitt answered it. She came into the kitchen, where the others were eating breakfast, looking puzzled.

"It's Granny Enders," she said. "She wants to speak to Amy. I do hope she's not going to make trouble at the last minute."

Amy ran down the hall, her skin prickling with excitement. "Hello," she said breathlessly.

"Amy," said a familiar voice, "get me a broom. I've had mine in the cupboard so long there's dry rot in it. I wouldn't fly far on this. Go to a shop and pick out a good one.

"But wouldn't it have to be a special type?" asked Amy, confused.

The old lady at the other end of the line began to laugh. "No," she said. "Any sort will do. It's a prop really, for balance and comfort. Flying is all in the mind. Get it today and come round here with the others."

Amy went slowly back to the kitchen, thinking hard. Everyone looked up eagerly, especially Mrs Pitt. "What did she say?" they all asked.

"She wants to see us again before we go ...
just the children," said Amy. "Can we go round
this afternoon, Mother?"

"Yes of course," said Mrs Pitt, still looking
worried. "Do be careful not to say anything to
annoy her though, won't you?"

As soon as the children were alone Amy
said quickly, "Have any of you any pocket
money?"

She explained what Mrs Enders wanted.
They counted their coins carefully and the total
was one pound and fifty new pence.

"I hope that's enough," said Jean. "Was
there a hardware shop on the way to Granny's?"

"Yes, about four doors away," said Peter. "I
noticed it last time."

The shop was just where Peter remembered
it. They stood on the pavement and looked at
the teapots, the cutlery, the garden shears and
boxes of nails displayed in the window.

"I can't see any proper brooms," said Amy,
worried. "Just those broom-heads in the corner
there."

"Perhaps we could nail one on to a handle,"
said Peter dubiously. He was remembering an
occasion about six months before when his
father had tried to do just that and managed to
split the head right across the top.

They went into the dark little shop and made
enquiries.

"No," said the untidy little lady behind the
counter. "No, I have no broom handles. They'll

38

be in next week. The only complete brooms I have at the moment are the plastic ones with nylon bristles."

She disappeared into a back room for a moment and came out with a pastel-coloured armful. The children peered doubtfully at the three brooms as they stood leaning against the counter — yellow, pink and green.

"They don't look very suitable," said Jean hesitantly. "We're buying it for a very old-fashioned lady you see."

"But these are splendid," said the shop-keeper indignantly. "They're very strong. I use one myself — those long silky bristles are splendid for moving the dust and they wash beautifully!"

She picked up the yellow broom, moved round the counter and began to sweep the floor vigorously. Clouds of dust arose and the children coughed. Jean remembered that their mother had asked them not to be away for long. There were plenty of last-minute jobs to be done at home.

"Perhaps the pink one would do. How much is it?"

"One pound and thirty p."

The lady carefully wrapped the broom in several lengths of striped paper, while Jean counted out the silver.

"Only twenty p. left out of our pocket-money," mourned Peter.

They reached Granny Enders' door and

found it closed. They twisted and pulled at the knob, but it seemed to be locked.

"Up here!" said a harsh voice, over their heads.

They looked up and saw Mrs Enders leaning out of a very high window, looking most annoyed.

"You're late!" she shouted above the noise of the traffic, "and I'm too busy to let you in. Time is very short!"

Amy waved the broom at her desperately. "We brought what you wanted," she called.

Mrs Enders gave a brief nod, then she pointed to the end of the street. A small horse was standing peacefully in the gutter, fastened to a cart, unworried by the cars and the crowds on the pavements. He belonged to the rag and bone man and was the only horse left in the district, so the children always enjoyed seeing him quietly clip-clopping along.

Suddenly, as Granny pointed, he began to rear and whinny, smashing his hooves up and down on the road. An old chair slid off the back of the cart with a crash and everyone turned to look.

While they were all staring at the horse, Amy felt the long slim parcel in her hand give a gentle tug, then it sailed noiselessly up into the air — up and up — straight into Mrs Enders' outstretched hand.

No strangers noticed anything. The other children heard Amy's soft gasp and looked in

time to see Granny catch the broom.

The window above them shut with a slam and they walked home, wondering.

"She didn't even say thank you," said John indignantly.

Next morning they stood in the hall waiting for the taxi to take them to the boat train. It was snowing lightly outside and Mrs Pitt made them button up their coats and put on scarves and gloves.

Amy slipped upstairs, pretending to go to the bathroom, but instead tiptoeing into the bedroom.

The little cat still sat upon the wallpaper.

"Candar," she whispered. "We're going! We have to go to the train!"

The picture on the wall did not move and sadly Amy went downstairs.

The taxi arrived and they climbed inside. Mr Pitt helped the driver to load their overnight bags into the boot. Most of the luggage had been taken away a week before. Amy stared miserably out of the window as the car turned into the traffic and the other children were depressed too. They thought of Candar, left alone in the empty house. Without him, how could Granny Enders travel?

Suddenly Mrs Pitt said, "Why Amy, what a pretty brooch! Wherever did you get it?"

Everyone looked at Amy's coat in surprise. Pinned firmly on the right lapel and dusted with a few melting snowflakes was a little copper brooch shaped like a cat. The copper shone like gold on the cat's body and darkened at its face, tail and the ends of its paws. The eyes were two glittering little blue stones.

None of the children doubted for a minute where it had come from. Smiles spread around the taxi.

"Wherever did you get it?" asked Mrs Pitt again.

Amy swallowed and wondered what to say but Jean replied quickly, "From Granny Enders," which was true anyway.

"How very surprising," said Mr Pitt. "I've

never known her give anyone a present before. She must like you, Amy.''

The traffic was thick and snow blurred the windscreen but the taxi threaded its way slowly across London. Then came the train ride.

At last they were waiting in the big customs hall with their luggage beside them. One man examined their passports and tickets, another marked all their bags, even Mrs Pitt's handbag, with chalk crosses. They hurried up stairs and along corridors and there was the ship, huge and white, waiting alongside the quay. They walked up the covered gangplank, a little dry tunnel with the snow falling thickly outside it.

The Journey Begins

Inside the ship it was warm and the narrow corridors were full of people looking for their luggage or saying goodbye to friends.

A steward in a white coat showed the Pitts their cabins. The children had a cabin with four bunks and their parents a double cabin a little further along the corridor.

"I wish we were next door to you," said Mrs Pitt, "in case anyone is ill in the night. But if anything goes wrong you can easily come and tell me, Jean. It's only a few steps down the corridor."

"Yes, of course," said Jean quickly. She was thinking that since Candar was with them it was maybe as well that their parents were a little way away.

The cabin was a very small room for four people and every centimetre was planned and precious. The children poked around, admiring the neat cupboards tucked into odd spaces and the way the upper bunks folded against the wall to give more space during the day. There were shelves and seats that folded down also and little rails to stop people falling out of upper bunks and glasses falling into the washbasin. There was also a little round porthole.

The children hung their coats in the narrow wardrobe and went off to explore the ship. Amy unpinned the little cat from her coat and fastened it to her jumper. The brooch had a long, gleaming, sharp pin and a strong safety-catch.

"I'll sort out the luggage while you're away," said Mrs Pitt, relieved to have space to spread out the cases and open them.

The children walked the ship from end to end. There were two big rooms reserved for adults only, and passengers were not allowed to go down where the crew lived, but they explored everywhere else. They found the two swimming pools, empty in port, with protective nets tightly drawn over them. It was too cold to stay out on deck in the swirling wind anyway. There was a huge playroom for the younger children with small chairs and tables and cupboards full of games and toys. There was also a slippery-dip, a roundabout, a climbing frame and a cubbyhouse with real curtains at the window and a toy cooking-stove inside it. John and Amy decided to come back and try everything later.

They looked at the library, the reading rooms and the writing rooms, where no one was allowed to talk. They stared through the locked glass doors of the enormous dining-rooms and saw the table stewards bustling around, setting the tables for lunch. They tried the chairs in the big lounges and peeped into bathrooms and showers.

They were not allowed to use the lifts without an adult so they pattered up and down hundreds of stairs and along endless corridors lined with the numbered doors of other people's cabins.

"Don't run!" said Jean anxiously to Peter and the twins. "We could easily trip people up."

From time to time Amy stroked the little brooch and whispered, "Did you see Candar? Isn't it exciting Candar?"

"I'd like to see the games deck and the sun deck," said Peter, so they went right up to the top of the ship.

They stepped out on to a deck sheltered by big glass screens. The boards were marked out into courts with nets stretched across them.

"This is for playing deck tennis," said Peter. "Look at those rope rings. You throw them back and forwards over the net. And those rings painted on the floor are for deck quoits. You try to throw the rings to the middle of the circle."

The twins wanted to play then and there but they were all shivering without their coats and in spite of the shelter of the screens the deck was slippery with melting flakes of snow. Jean managed to persuade them to come back into the warmth of the ship.

They returned to their cabin finally and Mrs Pitt looked up from piles of clothes and suitcases to say: "Goodness I'm glad to see you. I'd no idea where you were and the children's lunch is in ten minutes."

She explained that there were too many people on the ship for everyone to eat at the same time so some people were served at 12.30, some at 1.30, and the children had a special mealtime at 11.45. Everyone had a special place on a particular table and must always keep to this.

There was a frantic scurry to comb hair and wash hands. The gong sounded and they all went down for lunch.

The tables were spotless with stiff white cloths and gleaming cutlery. There was a menu from which you could choose all sorts of things to eat. Amy was drinking her soup very carefully, so as not to spill a drop, when suddenly she had a shock. Something warm and furry pressed against her leg. With her heart thumping she carefully put down her spoon and looked at her jumper. The brooch had gone. The fur pressed against her leg again.

"Amy! For the third time — what would you like for your main course?" demanded Peter.

Candar bit her leg gently. "He's hungry too," thought Amy. "I'd better get something that won't make a mess." She looked wildly at the menu.

"Amy, do hurry! How about fish with tomato sauce?" said Jean, embarrassed, as the steward stood impatiently at the end of the table.

47

"No — I'd like cold roast beef please." The steward went away and Amy was able to whisper to the others: "Candar is under the table."

When the beef arrived she made a little screen of salad at the end of her plate and waited for a time when no one at the other tables was watching her. Candar was getting restless. She felt a claw delicately prick her leg. She slid a slice of meat from under a lettuce leaf and slipped it under the table. It was snatched from her hand. She wondered if it would be enough. It was a large slice of meat.

Evidently it was enough. She felt no more pin-pricks and no more fur brushing her leg.

Once the steward bent down to pick up a fork that John had dropped and the children held their breath but the cloth hung well down over the sides of the table and the man noticed nothing unusual.

At last the meal was over and they looked at each other undecided. They couldn't walk out and leave a cat under the table. Amy slipped her hand under the tablecloth and felt around. Suddenly something was placed gently in her palm and she closed her fingers around the little brooch.

"It's all right now," she said breathlessly, "I have him!" She quickly put the brooch in her pocket.

Shortly afterwards Mr and Mrs Pitt went down for their own lunch and the children were alone in the cabin without fear of interruption. Mrs Pitt had filled the neat little drawers and wardrobes with their clothes and hung their dressing-gowns on the hooks on the back of the door. The empty cases were stacked in the corridor ready to be taken down to the baggage room. There was a little plastic stool with a fitted cushion in the cabin and Amy laid the brooch on this. They stood around and stared at the small copper cat and the glittering blue eyes looked emptily back at them.

"It's all right, Candar. We're alone. You can talk to us now," said Jean urgently, but the little brooch just lay there. It was hard to imagine it had ever been anything else.

Suddenly the ship's hooter sounded loudly. "We're sailing!" Peter said excitedly. They had heard the announcement ordering visitors ashore when they were in the dining-room but had forgotten that the departure time was so close.

"Let's go up and watch," cried John. They pulled on their coats and dashed up on deck, Jean carefully locking the door behind them as her mother had told her to do.

It had stopped snowing but little pools of freezing slush lay around the deck and the wind was biting. They leaned on the icy rail and watched the tugs butting, pushing and pulling at the sides of the liner. Not many people waved from the grey quay in the bitter weather. They had said their goodbyes earlier in the warmth of the ship or the customs hall and now they had gone back towards their warm houses.

Past all the other ships anchored in the port the tugs escorted the liner to the open sea. The ship hooted to them and they hooted goodbye and set back to the shore. The pilot who had been on board to help take the ship out climbed down a swaying ladder into his smart little launch and waved. The ship moved steadily out to sea and all the children could see now was grey sky and grey waves.

Gently the deck began to toss up and down. "I wonder where Granny Enders is," said Jean. They walked round and round the decks staring up into the sky but all they saw was a few seagulls. "I'm absolutely frozen," gasped Amy at last. "Let's go inside."

On their way along the corridor they heard their parents, back from lunch, talking behind the closed door of their own cabin.

"They're starting their unpacking now," said Peter. "It should take them quite a while." They unlocked the cabin and when they saw the Siamese cat curled up on the stool they slipped through the door and closed it as quickly as they could.

"Candar, you'll have to be careful!" said Jean anxiously. "Suppose the cabin steward had been in to bring some towels or something."

Candar looked at her haughtily. "I'm always careful," he said, "and I have very good ears. For instance — your father is coming now. Open the wardrobe door." John hastily tugged open the door of the wardrobe and the cat jumped smoothly inside.

The children strained their ears but could hear nothing at first. Then came a light footstep on the soft vinyl tiles outside and their father opened the door a little and put his head into the cabin.

"Your mother's still unpacking her things," he said, "and I'm going to walk around for a bit. Any of you coming?"

"We thought we'd like to rest for a while," said Jean awkwardly.

Mr Pitt looked most surprised. "That's rather unusual," he said, "but it's a good idea. You were all up very early this morning." The sound of his feet died away along the corridor.

Amy ran to open the wardrobe door. Candar was lying comfortably on a lifejacket on the floor of the wardrobe. "This will be a good place to sleep," he said. "Ventilation holes and everything! I've had rather an exhausting morning." He curled round, tucking his nose under his tail, and closing his eyes. The children looked helplessly at each other. Jean gently closed the wardrobe door. "He doesn't tell us much does he?" she said.

"We'll have to take turns to feed him," said Amy. "I didn't have enough lunch."

"You should have ordered something else as well," said Jean. "You can have as much as you like on a ship. But of course we'll take turns if you like. John! When it's your turn order something sensible. We daren't drop minced beef on the floor, for instance."

"I don't particularly enjoy eating off the floor anyway," said a cold voice from the wardrobe. "You must find me a dish from somewhere, then you can give me icecream. I'm very fond of it."

"We're going to have to be careful." Peter was looking worried. "Can you imagine what would happen if they found a cat under the table?"

"No," said John. "What would?" They were silent, thinking about it.

The door opened suddenly and Mr Pitt appeared. "There's a big bird flying behind the ship," he said. "Perhaps it's an albatross — but it's too far off to see clearly."

The children dashed past him along the corridors and out on to the deck at the back of the ship. It was tossing quite noticeably now and the sky was dark and stormy. The wind stung their cheeks and the white churning wake spread like a broad ribbon behind them. At first the sky seemed empty, then they noticed the white dot moving clearly against the grey clouds.

"It's a long way off," said Mr Pitt, behind them, "so it must be a pretty big bird." He shaded his eyes with his hand as the spray was stinging them. "Do you know ... I think it has pink legs."

"Not pink legs," whispered Peter to the

others, "just a pink plastic broom!" They doubled up with laughter.

"Inside now," said Mr Pitt, briskly. "You'll catch cold without your coats."

They went back to their cabin and when Amy was sure that her father was not following them she opened the wardrobe door and stroked the cat.

"Candar, wake up!" she said. "We think Granny Enders is following the ship. Shouldn't you be out there helping her?"

Candar opened one eye and looked at her. "I am helping her," he said. "I don't need to sit on the mast, you know." He went back to sleep.

On the Ship

When she woke the next morning Jean began to wonder if she was going to be seasick. The cabin seemed to rise in a curving arc then drop back, and each time she felt as though her stomach had dropped through the mattress. It was bearable if she lay back but if she lifted her head from the pillow she was very dizzy. The others were already scrambling round the cabin trying to get dressed. The floor was tossing and heaving and Peter fell backwards as he tried to open a drawer. Amy left the wardrobe door open and it flapped wildly back and forward, hitting John on the head. Mrs Pitt opened the door and looked at the chaos.

"Jean," she said, "you look as if you need one of my tablets."

Jean swallowed the tiny pill with a little water and lay back gratefully. She had moved into the lower bunk where Amy slept in case she had to dash suddenly to the bathroom.

"Just relax and keep still," said her mother. "That pill will fix you up but they take about an hour to work. I had one in the night and I'm fine now. Try and go back to sleep if you can. What a good thing it doesn't seem to affect the others."

The others were already down at breakfast. Jean lay uneasy and miserable. Several times she thought she must get up to be sick, but she was terribly drowsy and presently she fell asleep.

She was woken by Peter shaking her shoulder. "Jean, wake up! We think something awful's happened."

Jean opened her eyes, relieved to feel so much better, and saw three anxious faces.

"Granny Enders has disappeared. We can't see anything flying behind the ship. Perhaps she was drowned in the storm last night. Candar has gone too."

"I'll come up and look for myself," said Jean. She got up feeling rather weak and empty but no longer sick and hastily struggled into her clothes. "Let's look from the upper deck."

The ship was lurching badly. Out in the corridor they balanced first on one foot, then on the other, clutching at the rails that ran along the walls. Climbing the stairs was even more tricky. Amy felt that the sea was trying first to pull her back down the steps, then to throw her to the top. A woman struggled past them down the stairs looking very pale. "I think I'll be better lying down," she said to Jean. Jean nodded. She was pleased to feel all right.

They tugged open a door and scrambled out on to the deck. The wind hit them like a great, strong, wet sheet, whipped their hair to sting their faces and made John feel his ears would freeze. The children clung to the rail and watched the sea and the sky, their eyes narrowed against the wind.

"I wish I'd brought my gloves," gasped Amy peering at her red, wet knuckles.

The sky was dark and the waves lashed and tore at the ship sending a fine soaking spray all over everything. There were very few other people on deck and none of them stayed long. Canvas chairs which had not been stacked in time lay in pools of water and slid this way and that. There was no sign of anything in the sky, bird or witch.

"Perhaps she's hidden by the clouds," said Jean comfortingly.

"Let's have a look from the other end of the ship," suggested Peter. "She might be flying in another position."

They picked their way along the empty deck and came to the one sheltered corner on that side of the ship, where a glass screen angled from a cabin wall cut the force of the wind. An old woman was leaning back in a deck chair as if it was a warm sunny day. She was wrapped from head to foot in a thick, white fur coat. Her head was covered with a white fur cap with ear flaps and big white fur gloves covered her hands. It was Mrs Enders. The pink broom was propped behind the chair, its handle showing over the furry, white shoulder.

"Granny Enders! You're all right!" cried

56

Amy joyfully. "When did you get on the ship?"

"Last night. It was too rough by far. It's much better now and I'll be away before the weather clears and people come out in force. Though who's to know I'm not a passenger?"

"No one at first, I suppose," said Jean hesitantly, "but you look rather unusual you know ... striking," she added hastily, as the old lady glared at her. "No one would forget you very easily."

Mrs Enders appeared to be thinking. "I'm finding the flying a little hard," she said unwillingly. "It will be different when I get my herbs. I won't need you. I won't need the ship. I won't need anything! But for the time being I think I'll rest on the ship during the day, and fly at night. I'd be too conspicuous on board at night and there are no empty cabins. You'll have to bring me food from time to time. I couldn't carry much with me and I can't go into the dining-room if you all have special places. Just fruit and bread rolls! That's all I need. I don't eat much."

"What if Dad sees you," said John breathlessly.

"H'mm ... yes! I shall have to be careful about that."

A member of the crew walked past. He glanced curiously at the great white coat and nodded pleasantly to Mrs Enders and the children.

"There you are!" exclaimed the old woman

triumphantly. "He assumed I was a passenger right away — and why not indeed? There are far too many people on this ship for one person to keep track of them all."

She pulled back the great furry sleeve and glanced at her wrist.

"Ten-thirty. They are probably serving coffee in the public rooms and I'm going to have a cup."

The children watched nervously as she tucked the pink broom behind a ventilation pipe and made for the nearest doorway.

"We'd better go with her," said Jean.

"Where is the largest, busiest lounge?" demanded Mrs Enders in a ringing, confident voice. She seemed to have grown much taller since she stood up.

"Along here and down the stairs," said Peter quickly. The great white coat swept ahead of them down the corridor.

Stewards were pouring coffee at two large tables in the centre of the lounge. Mrs Enders swept up to one and loudly refused two cups because one was too weak and one was too strong. The third cup she complained was chipped. Finally she was given one to her liking. She had taken off her glove and the rings crowded on her fingers glittered and gleamed above the coffee cups. Everyone around the table was staring hard at her.

"I wish she wasn't quite so noticeable," thought Jean unhappily.

Mrs Enders swept off to a vacant table in the corner of the lounge and the children followed her thankfully.

"Good gracious! It's hot in here," she said. "Help me off with my coat, Peter."

Underneath she was wearing a red silk trouser suit with long flowing sleeves and a high neck. Down the front of the jacket were strange buttons studded with glittering stones. They looked like little faces and as the light sparkled on them their expressions seemed to change. The second button from the bottom grimaced horribly at Peter and he looked back, startled.

"Now what's the matter with you all?" said Granny Enders peevishly. "I've never met such children for staring."

"It's just that you don't wear the sort of clothes we usually see on grandmothers," said Jean nervously.

"Most grandmothers don't ride brooms! I assure you it's very awkward in a skirt! All my clothes are perfectly functional. This will be ideal for riding when we meet the hot weather — light and cool and perfect protection against sunburn."

She sipped her hot coffee thoughtfully. "This is splendid. Powdered milk I fear but much better than nothing. I don't see why I shouldn't enjoy this trip. Confidence is the key, children. I ask you — do I look like a stowaway?"

"What did you do about the plaster cast on your leg?" asked Peter curiously.

"I took it off. I didn't have time to go through all the rigmarole with the doctor so I sent him a note saying that I had gone to Edinburgh to seek better medical attention."

"Why Edinburgh?"

"Why not!"

Mrs Enders seemed to be getting annoyed and Jean thought perhaps it would be better not to ask any more questions for the time being.

"Let's have a game of Scrabble," she said. "I'll see if I can get a set from the games cupboard and Peter you go and get that little dictionary from the cabin. Then if we have any arguments about words we can look them up."

Amy and John were not old enough to play properly yet, but they leaned over the backs of the chairs, watched and gave advice. Peter explained to Mrs Enders that they each had seven little lettered tiles and had to form interlocking words on the scoreboard. Different squares on the board had different values and doubled or trebled the score for letters and words.

They played for a while with Mrs Enders scoring rather less than the others, then she triumphantly said, "There!" and arranged six letters over a triple word score — ZOBOXY.

"There's no such word!" said Jean and Peter together, before they could help themselves.

"A splendid score," said Mrs Enders pleasantly. "Of course there's such a word. Don't show your ignorance. That's a very small

61

dictionary but I assure you it will be in it."

Peter leafed hurriedly through the little book.

"It's not there," he said flatly.

"Let me show you," said the old lady with a gracious smile.

She stuck out her knobbly, thin, white, beringed finger and stabbed it at the page.

"There, Peter, there! Use your eyes!"

Peter stared incredulously. The word sat neatly and firmly on the printed page, spaced properly from its neighbours. He could have sworn it was not there a minute earlier. Wordlessly he passed the book to Jean.

"Well let's get on then," said Mrs Enders with satisfaction.

They played a while longer then Mrs Enders put down the letters QUAJY in a very advantageous position.

"Well — I've never heard of *that*!" exploded Jean.

"Look it up ... look it up ... I can see you all need some English lessons."

Jean opened the dictionary and there it was.

Suddenly, without saying a word, Mrs Enders rose to her feet, turned quickly, picked up her fur coat and hat and swept out of the room. The children were staring after her, surprised, when they heard their father's voice.

"Hello — I was wondering where you all were. How is the game going?"

He peered at the board. "It's no use fooling

around like that, you know. You must use proper words."

"But they are!" said Peter, "I saw them in the dictionary just now."

He turned the pages quickly. There was no ZOBOXY. Flushing, he looked for QUAJY. It had completely disappeared and the other printed words had closed their ranks leaving no gap in the smooth printed columns of the page.

He looked up at his father, feeling foolish and very angry with Mrs Enders.

"Just a joke," he said unwillingly.

"Well stop playing such nonsense and come up on deck," said Mr Pitt, getting to his feet. "The sun is out, the wind has dropped and some fresh air is just what you need."

They walked round and round the decks till their fingers and toes glowed and their cheeks tingled. At one sheltered corner on their rounds they always saw a figure muffled in a long white fur coat with big white gloves, lying back in a deck chair, apparently asleep. The white fur hat now had a thick veil tucked under it and it was impossible to see the lady's face.

Peter could not help it. On the fifth time round he bent down towards the figure in the chair and hissed, "You cheated!"

A high whining voice — unlike any they had heard Granny Enders use before — came from under the fur hat.

"Sir — can't you keep your children under control? It's very hard if an old lady cannot rest in a deck chair without being insulted by young hooligans."

Mr Pitt was furious. "I don't know what's got into you today, Peter," he snapped. "Apologise at once!" "I'm sorry," said Peter, feeling very injured.

They walked away. "Whatever did you say to her?" Mr Pitt asked. Peter sighed and didn't answer. He couldn't possibly explain.

"I think you'd better go down to the cabin," said his father, very much annoyed. "And if I hear of any more of this kind of behaviour there will be trouble I promise you."

Jean looked back along the deck. The figure in the chair was shaking with laughter.

The Arrival

The days passed quickly and the Pitts grew used
to the ship. John and Amy spent a great deal of
time with friends in the playroom. There were
many migrant families on the ship, going out to
settle in Australia, and most of them had several
children.

Peter and Jean found plenty of friends too.
They played deck tennis and deck quoits and
swam in the pool reserved for children. They
went to special film showings and the fancy-
dress party. All the time they kept their secret
about Candar and Mrs Enders. They decided at
the beginning of the trip that no one else must
know. Most mealtimes Candar rode to and from
the dining-room as a little brooch on Amy's
jumper. Under the table he consumed large
quantities of meat, fish and even icecream.

The children had bought him a glass ashtray
with a little picture of the ship on it, from the
ship's shop, and it made an excellent dinner
dish. Peter carried it down to the dining-room
each day in his pocket and brought it back in the
same way but wrapped in a paper napkin. They

washed it at the little basin in the cabin with hot water and soap.

Jean started to take her straw handbag to meals and into it she tucked fruit and buttered rolls, wrapped in a napkin, for Mrs Enders. The steward was amazed at the children's appetites.

After each meal Amy would walk round the ship with Jean's bag to find Mrs Enders and give her the food. She always seemed to find her much more quickly than the other children. She would pause and think and a picture would drift into her mind — the deck below the funnels, for example, or a corner of the sports deck, sheltered from the wind. She would go there and there would be Granny Enders, muffled in her furs at first, or as the weather became warmer, stretched out in her red trouser suit. Her face was always concealed by a tilted hat, a floating veil or a carefully-held newspaper, in case Mr Pitt should pass by.

As time went on Mrs Enders spent more and more time asleep during the day. Amy was afraid she was getting weaker. She began too to spend the evenings in various comfortable chairs in the public rooms. To the children's relief she did not join in the competitions and games organised by the entertainments officers. They were always afraid their father might notice her if she did anything too conspicuous.

Only late at night when nearly all the passengers had gone to their cabins did Granny Enders go to the stern of the ship, remove her broom from its hiding place behind the pipes and soar off into the dark sky.

Mrs Enders said goodbye to them the night before they reached Perth, in a dark, quiet spot at the stern of the ship where the great white wake roared and foamed behind them.

"We're very close to land and I don't want to be seen tomorrow. I'd better go ashore while it's dark."

"I hope you'll be all right," Jean said anxiously. She was surprised to find she had grown quite fond of the old lady.

Every day of the last week Mrs Enders had looked older and older. Her face was paler than ever and the skin stretched tightly over the bones.

"What if she can't find the plants she wants?" John asked miserably, as they watched the pink plastic broom disappearing in the dark sky.

"She hasn't any Australian money," said Peter, suddenly alarmed. "How is she going to get something to eat and somewhere to stay?"

"She'll manage," said Amy confidently. "I'm sure she still has enough magic left for the odd cheese sandwich."

"Wake up Jean, wake up!" She could feel someone shaking her shoulder. It was Peter.

"We'll be going through the Heads into Sydney Harbour in a few minutes. The steward told us to get up early."

The twins were already dressed and peering out of the porthole above the upper bunk. It was just beginning to get light and all they could see was a strip of grey land and a grey, gently heaving sea. Quickly Jean dragged on her clothes. As she opened the wardrobe to get her coat she stroked the smooth circle of fur on the life jacket.

"We're there, Candar!" she said softly, "at least, very nearly there. How are you going to get ashore?"

The cat opened one eye and looked at her, then closed it again and slid his nose under his tail.

"Do hurry up," clamoured John, dancing around. "He won't tell you. He never does! Come up on deck!"

Outside there was a cool breeze which made the children glad of their coats and the rail was cold and damp under their fingers. More and more sleepy passengers appeared on the decks, yawning, huddling into their collars and staring at the coast.

Amy looked up at the grey sky. "I wonder where Granny Enders is now?"

Slowly the ship slipped between the headlands and into the big harbour. The sky gradually lightened. The children swung on the rail and saw the shores, some steep and wooded, some crowded with patches of red roofs, and here and there a beach in a gentle curve below the trees. As they sailed further and further in, the sky reddened and at last they saw the bridge, stretching right across the harbour, and the Opera House, like a great ship with white sails, lying at the edge of the water.

The children's parents were up now, explaining and exclaiming and pointing.

It was already a very warm morning.

The Pitts had to wait a while in a huge shed-like building until a uniformed customs officer asked them if they had anything to declare.

"No," said Mr Pitt firmly, and they all looked the man straight in the face and tried to appear honest and harmless.

Jean thought about quarantine regulations for cats and her stomach felt rather hollow. The little brooch was again pinned to Amy's shirt. But he'd laugh at me, anyway, she thought. You can't put a brooch in quarantine.

The customs man looked steadily at them for a moment, paused, then signed each case and trunk neatly with a swirl of chalk.

Soon they were outside, on Australian pavements, under a clear bright sun, and Mr Withers, a representative of Mr Pitt's firm, was helping them into a very large white car. He loaded their hand luggage into the enormous boot.

"It may take till tomorrow to have the trunks delivered," he explained. "But if there's anything you need just ask me."

Mr Withers drove first through the crowded city, then through several suburbs with pleasant gardens and one-storey houses. Finally he stopped in the drive of the house where they were to spend their three years in Sydney. It was an old house, square and low, surrounded on three sides by wide wooden verandahs. Inside it was cool, rambling and dim because of the overhanging roof. The kitchen and bathroom had been modernised with shining surfaces and new equipment. Mrs Pitt was delighted.

The children rushed wildly around, exploring and arguing about who should have which bedroom. All the time the little brooch rode firmly and quietly on Amy's shirt — its blue, glittering eyes staring unwinkingly ahead.

The children went out into the large back garden, or "yard" as their Australian friend called it. It was a splendid place for games, mostly grass and shrubs with no tidy little flowerbeds to damage.

The Magic Yeast

It was late summer when the children arrived in Sydney. They started at the local schools a week or so later, and as the months went by they slowly began to feel at home. At the weekends they went for drives with their parents or with Australian friends. They visited the bush and all the beaches around Sydney. Sometimes they drove even as far as the Blue Mountains for picnics and barbecues.

All this time the little brooch sat silently on Amy's chest. Of Mrs Enders they heard nothing, though they looked for her everywhere they went. They searched the newspapers for mentions of strange occurrences. Sometimes they raced after some little old lady to look carefully at her face, but it was always someone else.

One rather cold, blustery Saturday morning Mrs Pitt started to think about baking bread.

"I'd forgotten about the public holiday on Monday," she said to Jean. "It will be a long weekend and we'll only have stale bread by Monday. Would you go up to the health food shop and see if you can get me some yeast?"

71

"All right," said Jean, "I'd like a walk, anyway." She slipped the money into her pocket and set off.

Just at the end of the road however she met some friends and they started to talk. An hour flew by and when she finally reached the shop it was almost closing time.

"I'm sorry," said little Mrs Beswick, peering at her over a mountain of dried apricots, "we've no yeast left. There was a run on it today. You might try the supermarket."

"I'd never get there before it closed," cried Jean in dismay. She hesitated outside the shop and wondered whether if she ran all the way to the supermarket she might be in time. An old woman, clutching a large bag, stood looking at the shop window with its neat pyramids of dried fruit and nuts and its huge assortment of cereals. She was bundled up against the cold with a scarf wound so closely about her head and neck that Jean could not see her face.

"If it's yeast you need," she said in a muffled voice, "I can let you have a little." She dived a hand into the bag, rummaged around and drew out a very small packet.

"Thank you," said Jean in surprise and relief. "How much do I owe you?"

"Take it as a present," said the faint voice, then with a low chuckle, "a surprise for your dear mother."

On Monday when Mrs Pitt was ready to

make the bread she unwrapped the yeast and looked doubtfully at it. There was very little of it and it had a pink tinge.

"I've never seen any like this," she said, "but I suppose it's all right. It ought to be enough for a kilogram of flour."

Amy helped her to measure the flour into a large bowl and mix in some salt. Then Mrs Pitt crumbled the yeast with a little sugar and mixed it into a well in the middle of the flour with half a cup of warm water. She scattered flour over this.

"Now we cover that with a cloth and keep it warm," she said, "and when the middle part cracks, the yeast will have started to work and can be kneaded up." She placed the bowl on a shelf over the radiator and started to grease a loaf tin. After about a minute Amy lifted a corner of the teatowel and peered into the bowl.

"It's no use looking yet," said her mother. "It will need at least ten or fifteen minutes."

"But it's cracking already," said Amy, "and bubbles are coming out."

Mrs Pitt put down her tin and came to look. The yeast was foaming up like a miniature volcano.

"I've never seen it happen so quickly before," she said. "Australian yeast must be different. I'll knead it up right away."

She melted a small piece of butter in some boiling water, then added enough cold water to give her a bowl of warm liquid. This she mixed into the flour and began to knead the sticky mass, punching and folding it. From time to time she dusted the dough with extra flour to make it easier to work and used a little flour to clean her fingers. After a while the dough was a smooth elastic ball.

"Now we keep it warm for about an hour," said Mrs Pitt. She carefully tucked the teatowel back around the bowl and placed it on the warm shelf. Then she started cleaning up the kitchen, putting things away in their proper places.

Amy wondered what to do during the next hour. She helped herself to a glass of milk from the fridge and drank it slowly, looking out of the kitchen window. When she turned back to put her empty glass on the sink she happened to glance at the bread bowl. There was a great swelling under the cloth.

"Mum . . . look at it!"

"This is absolutely amazing," exclaimed Mrs Pitt. "This will be the fastest bread I ever baked. Oh dear, we haven't even switched on the oven." She hurriedly set the dials.

"It will have to rise again after the second kneading," she said, "so the oven should be ready in time."

She tipped out the dough on to a large floured board and began again to punch and fold it. Instead of sinking into a smaller, pliable mass in her hands she had the sensation that the dough was continuing to swell. Soon there was no doubt about it. The more she struggled the larger it grew. Presently it was lapping over the edge of the board.

"Amy, get me the big bowl we use for the Christmas puddings," called Mrs Pitt wildly. "It's under the bottom shelf in the pantry.... Hurry!" She continued to punch and slap the dough, hoping to slow it down.

The other children were in the next room. Jean was reading and Peter and John were playing cards. Amy shouted to them to come and help her. The huge pudding bowl was very heavy and stacked full of smaller, little-used things — odd jars and pots, a spare whisk, a mincing machine and a large iron ladle. Quickly they unloaded it and carried it to the table. Jean hurriedly wiped it out with a damp cloth. Peter helped his mother to heave the big lump of dough over the rim. For a moment it lay there quietly, then its surface quivered slightly and once more it began to grow.

"It's bound to stop soon," said Jean. "It can't just go on and on. That bowl should be plenty big enough."

They stood round the table and watched in silence. Very, very slowly the dough crept up the sides of the bowl. When it reached the rim it seemed to stop for a while, then it started to swell again. First it bulged up into a mound and then it began to ooze over the sides of the bowl.

"Find something else to put it in," shouted Peter and they ran from room to room looking around them.

"We could put it in the bath," suggested John.

"You'll do no such thing," objected his mother quickly. "We can't possibly do without the bath."

They went back to the kitchen. The small table was now completely covered with a great heap of dough.

"I know!" cried Peter. "The new garbage bin!"

They had been the day before to buy a large, gleaming, new, yellow plastic bin. It stood outside the back door, still with a piece of brown paper taped round its middle and a receipt fastened to its lid. It had four little metal fasteners which snapped shut around the lid to

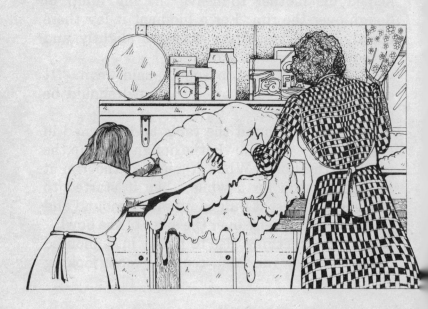

protect the contents from cats and dogs. Jean pulled it inside. "It looks very clean," she said.

"Well, we've no time to wash it anyway," said Peter.

They started to lift the dough into the bin, grabbing it from all sides. It stretched and billowed between them.

"Let's try cooking just a bit of it," begged Amy.

Mrs Pitt looked doubtful. "I can't imagine it being all right," she said, "but it won't go on growing in the oven. The heat will kill the yeast."

She seized a knife and cut off a chunk, then they pushed the dough into the bin. Peter put the lid firmly on and snapped the fasteners into position.

Mrs Pitt divided the piece of dough into two, kneaded the halves lightly, put them gently into tins and popped them in the oven. "With normal bread," she said, "you let it rise again, a little, before you bake it — but this might get away."

The oven had a light inside and a little glass window. Breathlessly the children watched the loaves rise like normal bread, then settle down to brown. Mrs Pitt reduced the oven heat slightly and sighed with relief. She was looking quite pale. "I used to make a lot of bread," she kept saying over and over again, "and I never remember anything like this."

The plastic bin began to rock — thump, thump, thump. The floor shook and a saucer

77

slipped from the draining rack and smashed in the sink.

"Perhaps if we tie it to something?" said Jean. "How about those hooks in the pantry?"

They dragged the bin to the little walk-in pantry. On the wall by the door were two large iron hooks. One held a string bag full of onions. Amy sat on the lid of the bin, patting it and making soothing noises. Peter searched frantically in a cupboard until he found a length of rope. Quickly they threaded the rope through two of the bin's fasteners and knotted it fast to the hooks. Amy climbed gingerly off the lid, still talking softly and giving the bin an occasional pat. It settled down quietly, rocking gently from time to time.

The bread in the oven turned out splendidly. At first they were uneasy about tasting it but it smelled so good and looked so ordinary that they all took a slice.

Mr Pitt came home while they were eating it and did not seem at all surprised at the story.

"It's just the good old-fashioned sort of yeast," he said. "Granny always used it when I was a child. You won't need to make any more dough. It just keeps on growing. Marvellous, really! I can't think why it ever went out of use. I've never seen any for years. Well, come to think of it, it was short even then. I wasn't allowed to show it to my friends in case the neighbours wanted some. Mind you, I used to think we could easily have supplied the whole street."

"I'm afraid to take off that lid again," said Mrs Pitt. "It's too hard to control."

"That's no problem," said her husband, cheerfully. "You just play some music, or even humming a tune will do. Perhaps the sound-waves interfere with its growth, or perhaps it just stops to listen. Then when the lid is safely back you can stop the music and the dough will fill the bin again."

"That old lady who gave you the yeast, Jean," whispered Amy. "What did she look like?"

"I couldn't see her face," said Jean. "It was all muffled up in a scarf ... but I expect you're right."

A Gift from Granny

Winter passed and the weather grew warmer. It was a beautiful spring with day after day of sun and only occasional wisps of white cloud hovering overhead. Light winds gently filled the sails on the harbour, there was no mud on the playing fields and tennis balls bounced cleanly on dry courts. Weddings and garden parties took place in unclouded sunshine.

It became hotter and hotter. To the twins there was only one drawback. When it was fine they ate their lunches in the schoolyard, which was sheltered by buildings on all sides. Usually this made a pleasant sun-trap but as the summer sun glared down the yard became too hot for comfort and the light reflected from the pale concrete hurt the eyes. Some children began to feel unwell and there were several cases of sunburn. On one of the hottest days the headmaster decided to keep everyone indoors.

"What we need out there," said Miss Whitton, Amy and John's teacher, "is a tree — a large, shady tree."

"Why can't we plant one?" asked a boy

called Gino Ponti. "It could go in that old flowerbed in the middle."

There was indeed a small, neglected circular bed in the centre of the concrete.

"An excellent idea," said a voice from the open door, and the headmaster, Mr Lumley, who had been passing, stepped inside. "What sort of a tree will it be? It will have to grow fast or it will be many years before we have any shade at all."

"It should be deciduous," said Miss Whitton firmly. "Children, that is how we describe trees that lose their leaves in the winter. We need the sun on the yard in winter. We don't want to shut it out."

"There are lots of little trees growing under the big one over the road," said Amy.

The headmaster thought for a moment. "No," he said, "that is a jacaranda and they are too slow-growing. Has anyone else any ideas?"

A girl called Penny Yates put up her hand. "Cherry plums grow very fast," she said.

"Yes," said Miss Whitton thoughtfully, "and they're very pretty but not I think quite large enough, and the little fruits would make a terrible mess in the yard each year."

Sue Tanner, who lived next door to the twins, waved her arm wildly. "Please Miss Whitton, Mr Lumley," she said, "there's a little rowan tree in the garden at home and Dad says we'll have to pull it out."

"Now that's a good suggestion," said the headmaster. "The Scottish rowan. It grows fast and it's very attractive, besides which it has an interesting history. Long ago in Scotland rowans were thought to have magical powers and they were planted close to the house to keep away evil spirits and influences. Perhaps we could do with a little protection here! Ha — ha — ha!" Smiling broadly he went back to his study to eat dried-up, curling sandwiches and drink warm lemonade.

Early next morning Amy and John met Sue outside her gate. She was holding a large pot. "Would you help me with my case?" she said. "I need three hands."

"Is that the tree?" asked John curiously, leaning forward to reach for the schoolcase. "It's very small." The plant seemed healthy but it was only about ten centimetres tall. The twins looked at it doubtfully. "It will probably grow very fast," said Amy comfortingly but she wondered privately just how long it would take.

They set off along the road with John grasping two cases and Sue carefully carrying the plant. They were just within sight of the school when a familiar figure suddenly sprang from behind a bush and glared at them, stabbing a bony, beringed finger at the plant pot.

"What are you doing with that thing?" snapped Granny Enders, for of course it was she. Amy and John jumped in surprise. They looked at one another, wide-eyed, both thinking at once how difficult it would be if Sue found out they had a grandmother in Australia when their parents didn't even know it. She'd be bound to talk about it at home — especially since Mrs Enders was such an *unusual* grandmother. But luckily Granny Enders made no sign that she knew them. All her attention was concentrated on the little tree in the pot, at which she was scowling ferociously. Granny looked very much better than when she had said goodbye to them on the ship. Her eyes were sparkling and her cheeks looked quite pink.

Sue, who had jumped backwards from the long, pointing finger, recovered and held out the pot. "It's a tree out of my garden," she said eagerly. "And we're going to plant it in the schoolyard so that it will be nice and shady in the summer."

"But that's a rowan!" snapped Mrs Enders. "Most unsuitable! You can't plant that. I won't hear of it." She suddenly leaned over, grabbed the pot from Sue's hands and with a shudder of distaste, tossed it on to the back of a passing lorry. The children shouted out but the lorry was out of sight in seconds.

"Why did you do that?" cried Sue, almost weeping, and staring at Granny Enders as if she was mad. "I told Miss Whitton I would bring it this morning — and it was a lovely little tree."

"What you need," said Mrs Enders, changing abruptly to a smiling, kindly figure, "is something interesting, like this." She bent down and groped under the bush. The branches heaved and parted and out slid a little tub with a small sapling in it. It was about a metre high and had a shiny red trunk and large, smooth, dark-green leaves.

"What is it?" asked John.

"You can look it up in a book in the school library," said Mrs Enders. "Though whether they're likely to have the right book I do not know." She leaned against a telegraph pole and roared with laughter. Then she turned and strode off down the street, without a backward glance. She had disappeared around the corner before the children realised what was happening. Amy ran after her, calling, but when she turned the corner there was no sign of Mrs Enders at all. She had completely vanished. Amy trailed back to the others.

"She's gone," she said flatly.

"Did you know that funny lady?" asked Sue wonderingly.

"Oh ... er ... no," stammered Amy. "I just wanted to thank her for the tree." She looked warily at the plant and wondered why she felt so uneasy. "Do you mind if we take this one?" she said to Sue.

"No," said Sue, who had cheered up. "I'd sooner take something, after promising, and it's a lovely size. It should grow fast."

There was a sudden, far-off clanging noise.

"We're going to be late," shouted John. "I can hear the bell."

"Quick," exclaimed Amy, trying to lift the tub. "Help me to carry it. I can't lift it."

It took the three of them all their strength to carry the plant. It really was amazingly heavy. Luckily some other children stopped to help them with their cases. The school bell continued to ring as they staggered slowly along the pavement, through the gate and down the long path. At last they reached the flowerbed in the centre of the yard and thankfully lowered the tub to the ground. Assembly lines were already forming and the children slipped into their places just in time.

After assembly a crowd gathered round the flowerbed and there was a buzz of conversation. "What a splendid plant," said Miss Whitton, coming over to examine it.

"An old lady gave it to us on the way to school," said Sue. "She didn't like the rowan."

"What sort of tree is it?" asked Gino.

"We don't know. She told us to look it up."

"And so you must," said Miss Whitton. "I'm very proud of the botanical section of the library."

It so happened that there was a library period that morning. Miss Whitton had been talking to the school librarian and when the children filed down to the library a stack of books was waiting on one of the tables.

"Now, we'll see who is the first to identify our new tree," said the teacher. "Take a book each. If there are not enough to go round, some of you can look through the geographical magazines and some through the encyclopedias." It was very warm in the library and very quiet except for the buzzing of a few flies and the rustle of paper. The books were all shapes and sizes, large and small, fat and thin, some with coloured illustrations and some with line drawings in black and white. The children sat, slowly turning the pages and looked at hundreds and thousands of pictures of plants. Sometimes a hand shot up and Miss Whitton hurried over to examine the picture, but she was never satisfied. "No Angelo — those leaves are the wrong shape. No Stephen, the stems don't divide in that way. Helena, I can't imagine why you think that is similar. Go outside and have another good, long look."

Amy had a large, heavy old book with thick, faintly yellow pages with roughly-cut edges. She worked slowly through the fine drawings, growing dazed at their number and variety. She did not expect to find the tree. She thought of Mrs Enders' laughter and felt sure the plant would not be in these books.

The library period came to an end. The books had been searched from cover to cover. Miss Whitton was surprised and disappointed. "Well," she said. "I should have liked to know if our tree needed special treatment but never mind. We'll plant it firmly and water it and hope for the best."

Some of the children wondered fleetingly why this tree was so welcome when no one knew anything about it. Miss Whitton did not seem to worry about its speed of growth or whether it would drop its leaves in the winter. Perhaps she was so eager for the school to have something unusual that she forgot to be cautious.

After lunch someone found a spade in the toolshed behind the main building and some of the biggest children took turns to dig a neat hole, roughly the size and depth of the tub. Then they found that they could not get the tree out of its container. The tub was built like a little barrel, with its staves held in position by iron bands. The earth held fast to the wooden sides and though they tapped it and shook it, it would not move.

"Loosen it round the edges with the spade," said John. But though the soil in the tub felt moist and crumbly it was impossible to drive the spade in for more than a few centimetres.

"Perhaps if we hold it upside down it will fall out," said Miss Whitton. "Come on now . . . four of you . . . be very careful, Sue, take hold of the trunk and tug it very gently." She began to thump the bottom of the tub as she spoke. It was no use. The little tree might have been sitting in a block of glue and it seemed heavier and heavier all the time. Hot and panting they turned it the right way up again.

"We must think carefully about this," said Miss Whitton. "We don't want to damage the tree."

Amy idly stretched out a hand and stroked

the side of the barrel, then jumped backwards as a burning, tingling feeling ran into her fingers and up her arm. Suddenly the staves of the tub fell apart like a loose pack of cards. The iron bands jerked off and clanged on the concrete, one of them hitting John on the ankle.

"What did you do Amy?" shouted Stephen. "It must have had a trick fastening."

They could see now that there had been very little soil in the tub — just a packed mass of twisted, brown roots. The children lifted the tree into the hole and firmed down the soil around it. John found a watering can in the shed and they took it in turns to fill this with water and sprinkle the ground around the tree. The earth was dry and powdery and soaked up the moisture like a sponge but after a while Miss Whitton decided they had done enough. "You have just time to wash your hands before the bell goes," she said. "And will two of you please put away the spade and the watering can."

The tree looked very much at home in the small circular flowerbed. Amy could almost feel it relaxing its roots and stretching out its shiny green leaves.

Miss Whitton took an expanding tape-measure from her pocket and swiftly measured the height of the trunk. "Ninety centimetres." she said. "I'll make a note of that and we must measure it frequently." The bell clanged for the first period of the afternoon and the children returned to their classrooms.

An Unpleasant Surprise

Next day, as soon as they arrived at school, John and Amy hurried to join the group around the tree. Miss Whitton was just putting away her tape-measure. "That's amazing," she was saying to Mr Lumley. "You were right. It has grown at least fifteen centimetres, overnight."

"Remarkable," said the headmaster. "This position must really suit it. Did you water it yesterday? The soil looks very dry." The children dashed back and forward with the watering can until assembly time.

Every morning was the same. The bed around the tree was always parched and dusty. No matter how they soaked the ground, the water quickly vanished. And all the time the tree grew steadily and noticeably. By the end of the week it had doubled its size.

The following Monday they were startled to find it was nearly three metres tall, already casting a useful patch of shade. Miss Whitton was beginning to look worried. "I wish we knew just what it is and how large it will grow," she said. "Still, we have plenty of room."

By the Tuesday of the second week, the tree

had reached a height of six metres. Mr Lumley stood and looked at it for a long time then he reached out and snapped off a leaf. "I'm taking this up to the University," he said.

An hour later the headmaster returned with the Professor of Botany and one of his staff. They seemed to be very excited. Amy's attention wandered from the maths lesson. Through the window that opened on to the yard she could see the visitors pacing all round the tree, waving their arms, measuring and making notes. After a while they went away, then returned with several of their colleagues. They stood talking and shaking their heads. Mr Lumley came into the classroom looking puzzled and pleased.

"No one knows what it is," he said. "We've created quite a sensation. It will be something interesting to show the Minister for Education when he comes to open the new block next week."

Miss Whitton did not seem so happy. That night after school she walked home with the twins to ask them about the old lady who had given them the tree. "I'm sorry," said Amy, in reply to her questions, "we haven't seen her since, and don't know how to contact her." That much at least was true, Amy thought guiltily. She didn't like telling fibs.

Day by day the tree grew. If you stood and looked carefully you could actually see the twigs lengthening; you could watch buds swelling from the new shoots and slowly opening.

An article appeared in the local paper with the headline, MYSTERY TREE PUZZLES SCHOLARS, and a picture of Sue standing under the tree in the schoolyard. "Just three weeks ago," said the article, "Sue Tanner carried this tree to school in a pot!"

The next day a television camera crew swarmed all over the yard and that night the children watched a news item on the amazing plant. "The question is," finished the announcer, earnestly, "where is the mysterious lady who kindly gave this astounding tree to the school? Will she please contact this channel as there are many questions we should like to ask."

The school routine was badly disrupted. Every day sightseers wandered in and out of the yard, talking and exclaiming. Their voices drifted through the classroom windows, open in the heat, making it difficult for the children to concentrate.

"Thank goodness the holidays will soon be here," said Mr Lumley, mopping his forehead after persuading some particularly persistent visitors to go home.

Then the afternoon arrived when the Minister for Education came to open the new wing of classrooms. Parents were invited to the ceremony, to be held in the yard. The children had been practising songs for a short concert after the opening and the Mothers' Auxiliary had been working all morning, preparing sandwiches and scones for afternoon tea.

The tree now formed a dense green canopy over the yard and cast a deep welcome shade over mothers in flowery dresses and floppy hats and fathers in summer shirts, over unnaturally neat children standing in tidy rows and teachers watching carefully for problems and disturbances.

The Minister made his speech and it was quite a long one — all about the history of the school and how he hoped it would develop in the future. Then just when they were all starting to feel rather sleepy, from standing still so long on a warm day, he said, "I now declare this new wing well and truly open!"

There was a tiny pause and people lifted their hands to clap, but suddenly there was a loud rending, cracking noise and a huge split appeared in the new building, zig-zagging from the ground right up to the corner of a first floor window. A great gasp went up from the crowd and then ... crunch ... snap ... and another great crack snaked through the older building on the other side of the yard.

"It's the tree," shouted one of the fathers. "It's undermining the foundations!"

Just then the ground seemed to heave slightly under their feet and a third crack appeared, close to the first one, with a noise very like a pistol shot.

"Clear the yard!" shouted Mr Lumley. "Get the children to safety. Don't panic, everyone, but get clear of the buildings as quickly as you can."

Chattering excitedly the crowd surged out of the courtyard.

"That tree will have to go!" shouted the Minister for Education. "There's no money left in this year's budget for new school buildings." He strode into the headmaster's office and made a brief, angry phone call. Shortly afterwards the wall of the office split from floor to ceiling.

In a very short while a truck roared into the schoolyard and it was loaded with men with chain-saws, axes and ladders.

The Professor of Botany, who had been invited to the ceremony, was pacing anxiously around. "Can't you spare the tree?" he begged. "It must be very rare and it hasn't even fruited yet, so we have no seeds." His words were followed by another loud crack and looking at the grim faces around him, he said: "Yes ... well ... I understand ... but at least let me photograph it." He rushed about, snapping the tree from all angles, while the men with the lorry waited impatiently. Then they set to work.

All afternoon they worked lopping the tree, and one by one the great branches crashed down on to the concrete below. Amy and John crept back to watch through a gap in the buildings. The Professor was wandering disconsolately around, taking samples of leaves and bark. "Perhaps we could grow it from a cutting," he muttered hopelessly, cramming the twigs into his pocket. "Get out of the way!" shouted a workman frantically, as yet another branch crashed down beside him.

At last only the huge, crippled trunk was left, with gashes all down its sides. There was a careful discussion about how to fell it safely, then the chain-saw bit into the smooth, red bark. First they cut a wedge from one side of the tree, then they started to cut through the trunk from the other side. Finally there was a loud tearing and cracking and the tree dropped neatly between two buildings.

"The summer holidays will have to start early for this school," said the Minister gloomily to the headmaster. "Let's hope we can repair the damage."

For two days the workmen toiled cutting up the wood from the tree and carting it away. All pensioners with open fireplaces were given free loads to keep for the winter.

The Day of the Fire

One hot summer morning in the school holidays Amy woke up excited and restless. She had the feeling that something was going to happen. Quietly she slipped out of bed, tiptoed out of the room she shared with Jean and padded on bare feet to the kitchen.

A cat was sitting on the doormat, peering through the flyscreen door at a kookaburra on the tree outside. It was a creamy-coloured cat with dark shadings along its back and still darker ears and tail.

"Candar!" cried Amy joyously. The cat yawned, stretched and rubbed lazily round her legs.

"She's coming today," he said in tones of great satisfaction. "Give me something to eat. I'm starving!"

"Who's coming? Mrs Enders? How do you manage for food when you're a brooch or a picture?" said Amy breathlessly as she picked the silver foil top from a bottle of milk and poured the cream gently into a saucer.

Candar took a few laps and paused thought-

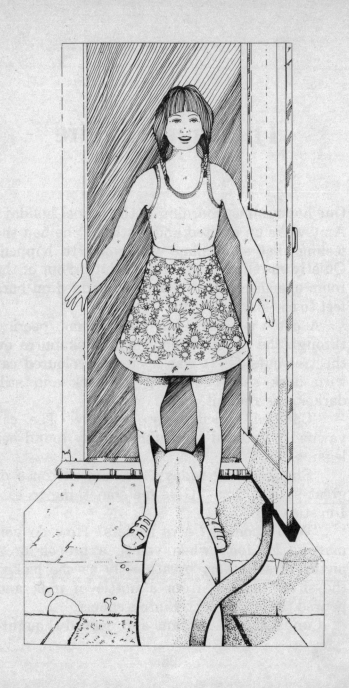

fully. "There are some things," he said, "which defy explanation."

"I suppose I'll have to be satisfied with an answer like that," thought Amy, rather resentfully. She opened the door of the fridge to replace the milkbottle and slipped a slice of cold chicken from a plate on the top shelf.

"Amy!" cried her mother's voice. "Wherever did that cat come from? And why are you giving it our chicken?"

Amy jumped and dropped the slice of meat. Candar pounced on it and it disappeared swiftly. "He seems to be lost," said Amy hurriedly, "and he's awfully hungry."

The cat washed his nose delicately, smiling behind his paw. He strolled over to Mrs Pitt and rubbed around her legs, purring in an ingratiating manner. Louder and louder grew the sound, filling the room like the throb of a small engine.

"It's most peculiar!" exclaimed Mrs Pitt, bewildered. "I could swear this is the same Siamese cat we had in London, but it couldn't possibly be. I suppose they all look very much alike. Ah well," she said, tickling Candar behind the ears, "we'll have to try and find out where he belongs."

The rest of the family soon appeared. Mr Pitt was thinking about problems waiting for him at the office that morning and hardly noticed the cat. The children were very excited and kicked each other continually under the table.

At last breakfast was over and they ran out into the back yard with Candar sauntering behind them.

"He says someone's coming!" said Amy, as soon as they were out of earshot of the kitchen.

"Is it Granny Enders? Has she found her herbs?"

"Perhaps," said the cat, irritatingly. He streaked across the lawn, and up the coral tree, where he lay stretched along a high branch in the shade.

Though only early morning it was already very warm indeed and a dry, hot wind was blowing from the west. The children blinked in the sunlight and peered up at Candar but he stayed motionless. They watched for a while but soon became very uncomfortable in the hot wind.

"It's awful out here," complained Jean. "Let's go and have a game of Monopoly in one of the bedrooms, where it's coolest."

The wide old verandahs made the house rather dark but they also helped to keep it cool on days like this. The children sat in a circle on the floor in the shaded bedroom with the Monopoly board in the middle. The windows were all tightly closed to keep the house as cool as possible. They found it very hard to concentrate on the game.

After a while Candar disappeared from his tree, which they could see from the window, but when they went out for a brief search they could not find him. They went back to the game but somehow it was not as interesting as usual.

Over lunch, which was salad and icecream, Mrs Pitt looked worried and preoccupied.

At last she said, "I've been listening to the radio and bushfires are spreading around several suburbs. I wonder if we're in any danger here. That patch of bush at the end of the garden stretches right back to the National Park, and there are fires there."

After lunch it grew hotter and hotter. The children lay around listlessly on their beds, reading and sucking iceblocks. The air inside the house had warmed up considerably but it was still cooler than the scorching garden outside. Candar seemed to have completely vanished.

About three o'clock there was a pounding on the front door and they all ran into the hall. Their neighbour, an old man called Mr Mather, was standing there in a faded shirt and a pair of shorts.

"I can smell smoke," he said, "and I think the fires are coming this way. The brigades are all busy so we'll have to do what we can. Luckily the gardens are long between the bush and the houses, but you'd better plug the downpipes and run a hose into the gutters."

He showed them how to stuff old clothes and rags into the downpipes to block them, then to fix the garden hose so that water ran into the gutters around the roof. As the gutters filled the water could not get away down the pipes, so it overflowed, surrounding the house with a glittering curtain.

"That's fine," said Mr Mather, turning off the tap. "If the fire gets close, switch on the water. And keep your eyes open for blazing twigs blowing into the garden. You might be able to beat them out before the shrubs catch alight."

The children were alternately excited and frightened. They ran around looking for thick gloves and strong sticks in case they had to help fight the fire.

Mr Pitt arrived back in his car from the office, worried by the radio reports. "Perhaps we should get out of here," he said.

"Oh do let's stay," said Peter. "I'm sure we can save the house if we do."

"I'm told that with a strong wind these fires can travel very fast," said Mr Pitt. "They burn all the oxygen out of the air. I'm all for turning on the water and leaving now. Still, the gardens should be a good firebreak and our escape route's open. We'll give it a bit longer."

There was a red glow in the sky over the bush now and smoke reached the children on the hot wind as they stood in the garden and stared in the direction of the fire.

"Go and get a few things together in case we have to leave," said Mrs Pitt. They ran into the house, snatching up their favourite treasures. Their mother took papers and money from the little drawer in the sideboard, and her jewellery from her dressing-table, and hurriedly slipped them into her handbag.

Mr Pitt went to check the water in the car radiator.

Suddenly in the middle of the confusion there was a loud ring at the front doorbell. John ran to open it, his mother close behind him. On the step, waving to a departing taxi, was a tall thin woman with silver hair and a long, flowing, brightly-coloured cotton dress. She turned to look at them and Peter saw the hooked nose and glittering eyes.

"It's Granny Enders!" he cried.

"It can't be!" said Mrs Pitt in confusion and embarrassment. (She had, you remember, never met Granny.)

"But it is!" said Mrs Enders, calmly. "Do ask me inside." She swept past them, along the narrow hall, and seated herself in the largest chair in the big sitting-room which stretched the width of the house and had windows at either end.

The other children came running, longing to ask questions. Mr Pitt came in from the back garden and seemed speechless with surprise. Finally he managed to say: "I don't know how you got here, Granny, but it isn't safe to stay. We may have to leave any moment now. The fire's getting much closer."

"Nonsense!" said Mrs Enders in a tranquil voice. She stretched out her legs and kicked off her high-heeled shoes, wiggling her toes luxuriously. They looked at her helplessly. She was very different from the frail old lady they remembered. She seemed about thirty years younger, her cheeks were fuller, her skin less wrinkled.

"You found your herbs!" said Amy joyfully. "You must have! Do you know where Candar is? He was here this morning."

Mrs Pitt was too preoccupied and anxious to puzzle about the questions. "You must come away with us now," she said urgently. "It just isn't safe to stay."

"Rubbish!" said Mrs Enders rudely. "The smoke is clearing."

They all glanced at the window and then stared in surprise. The sky was much lighter and only a faint haze hung before the window.

Mr Pitt wrenched open the back door and went to investigate. He came back a few minutes later. "I can't understand it," he said in bewilderment. "It's as hot as ever and the wind is still blowing towards us, but the flames seem to have turned away."

A small sleek shape streaked between his legs and leapt into Mrs Enders' lap. "I see you have my cat," she said, stroking Candar lazily. "Splendid! I'll take him with me."

"How could it be your cat?" began Mrs Pitt in confusion, but she had no reply and decided not to press the matter.

"Drinks!" cried Mr Pitt, who had been staring out of the window with great relief and pleasure. "Something cool for us all to drink! I'm so thirsty my lips are cracking."

He and Jean opened the frosty bottles of lemonade in the refrigerator and carefully filled the tall, fragile glasses they kept for special occasions. Jean handed round the lemonade on the large shining brass tray and everyone took a drink thankfully and sipped it politely. For a while there was silence then Mr Pitt said curiously: "You look marvellous, Granny ... years younger! How did you get out here? You must tell us all about it!"

Mrs Enders glared at him. "I shall tell you nothing!" she snapped. "Nothing whatsoever. You gave me no help at all and I owe you no explanations."

There was an awkward pause. "Well ... " said Mr Pitt uneasily, at last. "The danger seems to be over and there were one or two things at the office that really needed seeing to today ... I think I'll go back there for an hour or so. Can I give you a lift into town, Granny? Where are you staying?"

"Thank you, no," said Mrs Enders primly. "I have my own transport."

John looked thoughtfully out at the road — empty except for a neighbour's car.

"Will you have dinner with us Mrs Enders?" asked Mrs Pitt, nervously.

"Dinner? ... Why just dinner?" said the old woman, crossly. "Aren't you going to ask me to stay?" She laughed at the look of consternation on Mrs Pitt's face. "Don't worry," she said, "I was joking. I have interests to attend to. Just give me a few minutes alone with the children and I'll be on my way."

As soon as they were by themselves she smiled broadly. "I have come to thank you," she said. "And that's a thing I don't often do. I am really growing quite mellow. Everything is splendid! Just splendid!"

"You did find the herbs of course?" said Peter.

"Indeed I did, and much more beside. I have neglected this continent. It has great possibilities. Some Aborigines are helping me with the preliminary work. They know a great deal and have saved me a lot of time. From now on anything may happen here. Anything at all!" She laughed gleefully.

"Did you have something to do with stopping the fire?" asked Amy, breathlessly. "And did Candar? His fur smells quite smoky."

"What an extraordinary question!" said Mrs Enders. She rose from her chair.

"Is there a broom I can borrow?"

"I thought you said you had your own," said Peter, and received an impatient glare.

"There's an old thing from the toolshed," said Jean hurriedly. "I was going to use it to try and beat out the fire."

They went out through the glass doors with Candar behind them and found the broom leaning against the kitchen wall. It was very old and rather dirty, its broken bristles bunched with a rusty strip of metal. Mrs Enders eyed it distastefully.

"It will just about do," she said. "Children, you'll probably not see me again. I have a full programme ... though Amy perhaps has potential ... maybe ... later on." She mused for a moment then pulled a tiny ring from the little finger of her right hand and slipped it on to Amy's finger.

"Keep that," she said, "and we'll see ... perhaps. Go indoors now and don't look back for five minutes."

They went obediently through the glass doors and waited. When they at last turned round to look out at the garden, it was deserted.

They clustered round Amy to look at the ring. It was gold with a red stone that flickered with little lights as she moved her hand.

Just then their mother came in and she looked very white and shaken. "It must be the heat," she said. "I must have some aspirin and lie down. I looked out of the kitchen window and I thought ... "

"What did you see?" they all cried together.

"Nothing," said Mrs Pitt hastily. "It was just a bad turn. I need to rest." Rubbing her eyes she went off to the bedroom.

They went slowly out into the garden. By the toolshed there was a great swirl in the dust and at the edge of it a scattering of tiny paw marks. They stood for a while, staring up at the empty sky.

"I wonder," said John, "if we'll ever see her again?"

"Of course we will," said Amy.